Rabbit's

written by Pam Holden
illustrated by Lamia Aziz

1

A long time ago, rabbits did
not look like they do now.
They had small, round ears.
They liked to play tricks, too.

2

One day Rabbit went to play
a trick on the other animals.

Rabbit told Beaver, "The sun will go away after today. We will have no sun at all. Go and tell all the animals!" Beaver was not happy.

He ran fast to tell Mouse.
"We need to get food ready
for the bad days!" he said.
Mouse went to tell the other
animals the bad news.

Mouse told Bear that the sun was going away. He said, "It will be like night time all the time!"

Bear said, "We will be cold
and hungry with no sun!"
He ran to tell more animals
to get food ready.

Rabbit went into the long grass.
He saw all the animals running to
get food for the days with no sun.
That made him laugh. "I like to play
good tricks! This is fun to see!"
he said to himself.

Moose came to see his friends.
They were all running to get food.
They told him the bad news.
Moose said, "Who told you that?"
"It was Rabbit," they said.
Moose told them that it was a trick.
"Rabbit likes to play tricks," he said.

The animals went to look for Rabbit.
Bear saw him in the long grass.
He got him by his small, round ears.
Bear pulled him up, and all the
animals laughed.

Bear pulled Rabbit's small
round ears for a long time.
The animals all told him that
they didn't like his bad trick.

Rabbit said that he was sorry.
Bear put him down and let go
of his ears.
His ears were long now!

Rabbit was happy that his new long ears were better. He never played bad tricks on the animals again!